MW01143226

Yoomee
and the Wonder Team

Written and Illustrated by
DR. "W"
Ray G. Wilkins, DCH
Edited by Patricia Wilkins and Kathleen Isaac.

Dr. W's two basic rules:

RULE NUMBER ONE
"All children have the absolute right to unrestricted love."

RULE NUMBER TWO
"We are all children."

Published in the United States by Red Carnation Training Institute
10924 Mukilteo Speedway, Suite 171, Mukilteo, WA. USA 98275.
1 800 561-1085 (206) 355-3647
Project coordination and production by STRATEGIC BUSINESS RESOURCES (206) 862-8456

ISBN 0-9648290-0-2
Printed on recycled paper in Seattle Washington.

L

et's begin by taking a deep breath

in through your nose.

Hold it in to the count of four.

Now let the air out slowly through your mouth.

Just sit back, relax and quietly listen as I tell

you the story of YOOMEE and the Wonder Team.

This is the story of a beautiful

little girl named YOOMEE. She lives just a few

miles from here. She loves her family,

she loves her friends, she loves her pets and they

all love her. That makes YOOMEE very happy

because we all need to be loved.

ot too long ago,

YOOMEE was not very happy

at all. In fact, she was very sad.

Let me tell you what happened.

As I'm sure you can see from her picture,

YOOMEE has skin and hair of many colors. Some of the kids

at her school couldn't see how beautiful YOOMEE was. All

they could see were the colors of her skin and hair. They

laughed at YOOMEE and teased her. They didn't take the

time to get to know her. They didn't even talk to her. They

just made fun of her because she didn't look like they did.

This made YOOMEE very sad. She began to cry.

As she walked home from school, she saw a beautiful rainbow of many colors. Next, she saw beautiful flowers of many colors growing along the road. YOOMEE thought to herself, "If I were a rainbow or a flower, the other kids would think my colors were beautiful. Why don't they think that people of different colors are beautiful? How boring it would be if the rainbow was just one color. How boring it would be if all the flowers were just one color. How boring it would be if all the people were just one color. We'd all look just alike! How boring!"

When YOOMEE got home, her Dad was

watching a football game on television. She watched

the game for awhile. She saw players of different

colors playing together as a team. The fans cheered

when someone made a good play, no matter what

color they were. YOOMEE wished that she was on a

team. But what kind of team could she be on?

The next day at school, YOOMEE noticed

that she wasn't the only one being teased. Kids

were being teased for all kinds of silly reasons.

But no matter what the reason was, the kids who

were being teased felt sad. Nobody likes to be

laughed at or teased. YOOMEE thought that there

must be some way to help kids who get teased.

Then YOOMEE had a wonderful idea. She

began to talk with some of the kids who were being

teased. They decided that they would start their own

team. They would start a team where nobody would

ever be teased. Their team would play games, be

friends and have fun together. Their team would help

people. They would call themselves "The Wonder Team."

Pretty soon YOOMEE's team began to have so

much fun. They talked about all sorts of things. They helped

each other with their school work and talked about interest-

ing books they had read. They became good friends. They

got to know each other. They listened to each other and

learned how much alike they all were. The team decided

they wanted to help even more people. They began to go

places together after school and help all kinds of people do

all kinds of things.

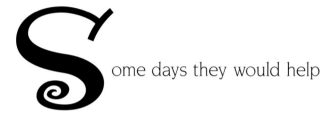

Some days they would help

serve food to homeless people.

They talked with the homeless people

and became friends with them.

It felt good to see them smile.

nother day they would

go to the park. They would help pick

up paper, cans and food that careless

people had thrown on the ground.

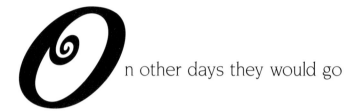n other days they would go

visit sick people in the hospital.

They would read stories to the sick people

and bring them flowers or drawings.

They even told them jokes and made them

laugh. Laughing seemed to be good for

people who were sick.

One day their team was visiting a

place where old people lived. They sang songs for

the old people and made them laugh. A television

news reporter was there. When he saw YOOMEE

and the Wonder Team doing so many wonderful

things, he asked them to be on television.

YOOMEE and her friends were very nervous. They had never been on television before. The camera lights were so bright. They told the television reporter all about being teased and how sad it made them feel inside. They told him how they formed their own team where nobody would be teased.

YOOMEE told him that the team had learned important lessons. They learned how to believe in themselves and how important it was to have good friends. They also learned that helping other people made them feel happy inside.

The next day YOOMEE and the Wonder Team were on

television and in the newspaper. They were even on the radio.

Kids from all over the country began calling YOOMEE and ask-

ing her how they could start their own teams. YOOMEE told

them, "All you have to do is learn to truly believe in yourself.

Then, you and your friends can begin to help the animals, the

Earth and people of all sizes, shapes, colors and ages. It doesn't

cost any money and it's so much fun!" It made YOOMEE so

proud that so many kids wanted to start their own teams.

That made YOOMEE very happy.

Thank you very much for listening.

Sample follow on discussion questions

Have you ever been teased?

Has anyone ever made fun of you?

How did you feel when you were teased?

What did YOOMEE do when she felt sad about being teased?

What are some things you can do when you feel sad?

What did YOOMEE'S Wonder Team do?

Would you like to be on a team like that?

How can you join a team like that or start one of your own?

What things would your team do?

What colors would you use?

What colors would you use?

37

What colors would you use?

About the Author

Dr. "W" has been working in the areas of education, training and counseling for over twenty five years. He has earned certificates and degrees in the areas of psychology, education, music, health, clinical hypnotherapy and counseling.

After teaching elementary school for six years, he has continued his work with children of all ages, including private and public entities, terminally ill AIDS clients, conference attendees, health and safety professionals, senior citizen groups, sales groups, wellness groups, and many others as a teacher, facilitator, counselor, writer and speaker.

With his multitude of experience, he offers suggestions not as a lecturing "expert" but as a guide or facilitator leading the listeners, students or readers toward their goals. His gentle, humorous, honest and simple approaches help his audience uncover the joy of "just being" and aid in the many discoveries along their "Wonderful Journey."

Please feel free to write us:

To order additional copies of this book
or for information about Yoomee's Wonder Teams
or to inquire about fund raisers and discount orders
or with any comments or suggestions about this book.

Published in the United States by Red Carnation Training Institute
10924 Mukilteo Speedway, Suite 171, Mukilteo, WA. USA 98275.
1 800 561-1085   (206) 355-3647